THE
FIRST FEUD

BETWEEN THE MOUNTAIN AND THE SEA

A FABLE BY
LYNN PLOURDE

PICTURES BY
JIM SOLLERS

DOWN EAST BOOKS
CAMDEN · MAINE

To Reagan, with love,
from Auntie Lynn

Text © 2003 by Lynn Plourde.
Illustrations © 2003 by Jim Sollers
All rights reserved.
ISBN 0-89272-611-3
Library of Congress Control Number: 2003106379
Printed and bound in China.
(RPS)

2   4   5   3   1

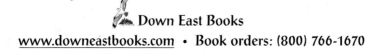

Down East Books
www.downeastbooks.com • Book orders: (800) 766-1670

Long ago, before people
   lived in the North Land and
began their own fighting,
      there was the first feud . . .

between the mountain and the sea.

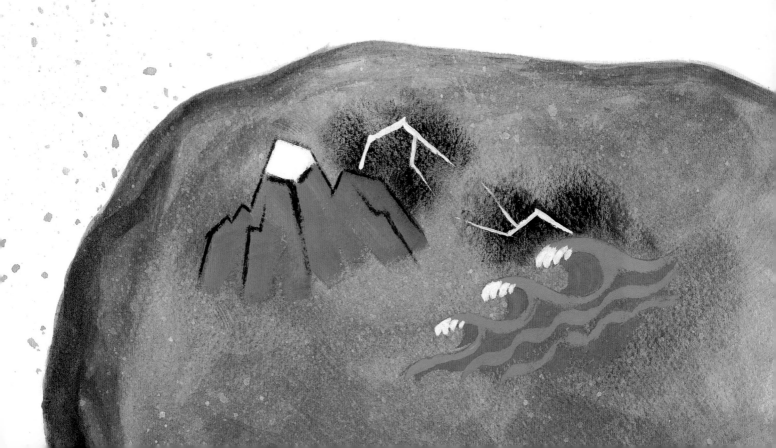

Katahdin claimed,
    "I am the greatest mountain,
        the most beautiful place in the North Land."

And, indeed, it *was* beautiful,
    with its majestic icy-white peak
        like diamonds stacked to the sky.

The Atlantic Ocean claimed,
"I am the most beautiful place in the North."

And, indeed, it *was* beautiful,
  with its shimmery swells like an endless sea of emeralds.

But Katahdin and the Atlantic
    were far apart and might never
    have heard each other's boasts . . .

. . . if it were not for the bald eagle
that traveled between them.

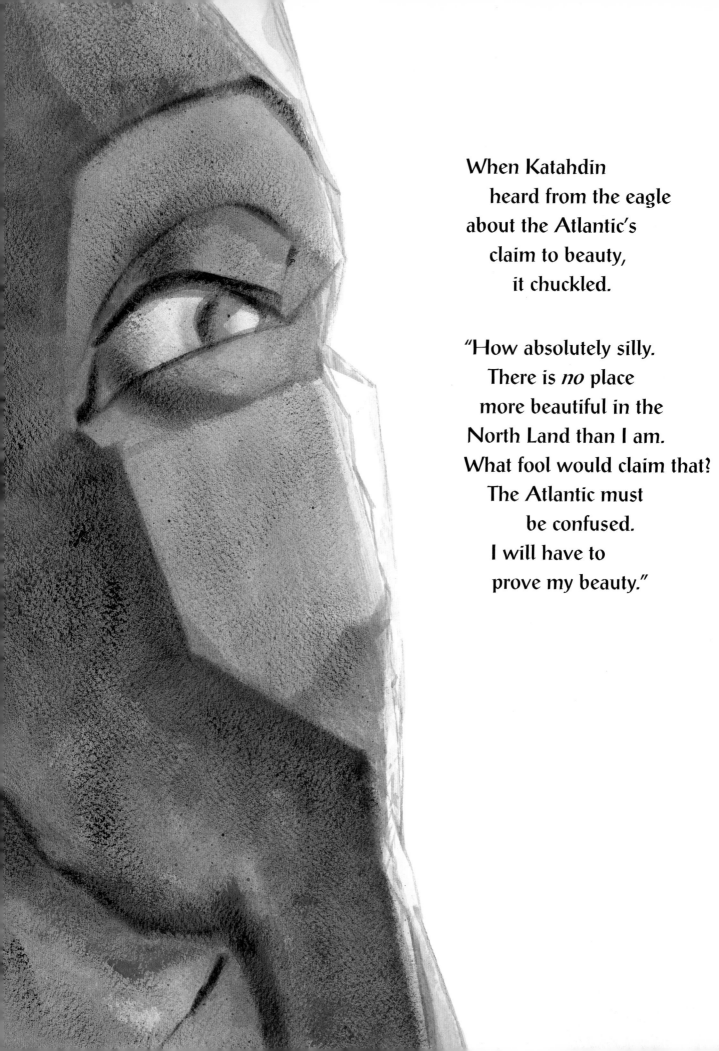

When Katahdin
    heard from the eagle
about the Atlantic's
    claim to beauty,
        it chuckled.

"How absolutely silly.
    There is *no* place
more beautiful in the
North Land than I am.
What fool would claim that?
    The Atlantic must
        be confused.
    I will have to
        prove my beauty."

And so the mountain
broke off a dazzling icicle
from atop its peak and sent
it in the eagle's talons
back to the sea.
"That will prove who
is the most beautiful."

But by the time the eagle arrived at the sea,
the icicle had melted away.

The Atlantic roared with laughter at the sight
of the few drops of plain, ordinary water
the eagle shook from its talons.

"Ho-hee-ha! That is all
Katahdin has to show for its beauty?
Poor, plain mountain.
I will show it
what *real* beauty looks like."

And so the Atlantic splashed
some of its sparkling,
foaming, bluish-green water
onto a floating leaf.

The eagle
carefully folded the leaf
with the water inside
and carried it back
to the mountain.

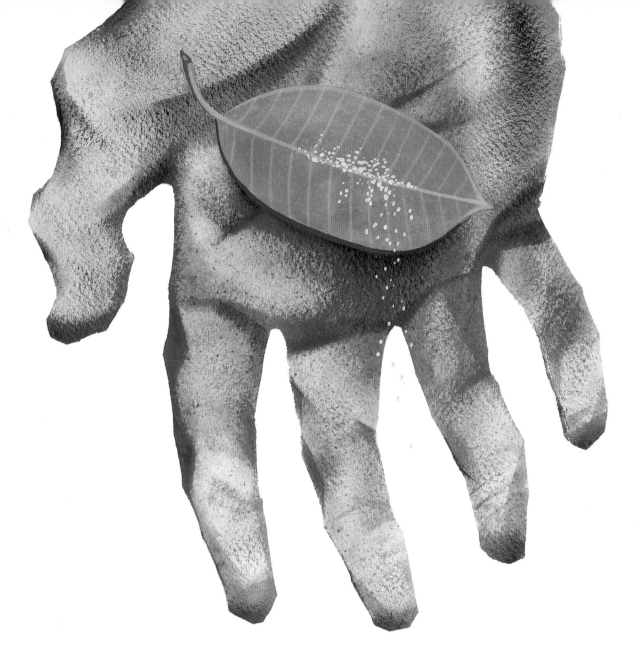

But by the time the eagle arrived at the mountain,
the ocean water had evaporated, leaving behind
only grains of sea salt upon the leaf.

"Plain, white powder—that is what the Atlantic thinks is beautiful?
Harumph!
I will show it true beauty once and for all."

And so Katahdin shifted and rumbled a bit in anger
and summoned the mighty, majestic moose
to be its messenger.

Katahdin wove its most dainty, delicate wildflowers
into a wreath for the moose to wear.
"Here," the mountain ordered, crowning the moose.
"Bring this to the Atlantic
and show it who is truly
the most beautiful
in the North Land."

But by the time
the moose had traveled

over the
mountain's boulders,

through forests,

and across coastal plains

to reach the Atlantic,

the fancy, fragrant
wildflower wreath had wilted
into a crown of dried brown twigs.

The Atlantic tossed and turned in anger.
"How dare that mountain insult me
with such a drab, ugly ornament?
It knows nothing, *nothing*
of true beauty."

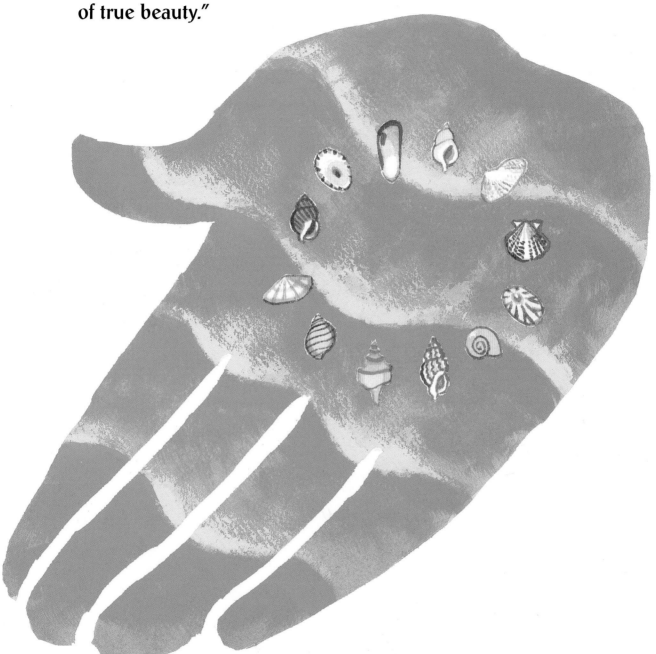

And with that, the Atlantic fashioned
a necklace made of its brightest, boldest seashells.
It placed the necklace around the moose's neck and ordered,
"Hurry, and bring this back to that mountain so that it may know,
once and for all, who is truly the most beautiful in the North."

Even though the moose
    tried to hurry back to Katahdin,
it could not help
    its naturally awkward ways.
By the time it arrived at the mountain,
    it had dropped the necklace
    many times and stepped on it twice.
All that remained were crushed shells.

"Enough is enough!"
shouted Katahdin
upon seeing the crumbled pieces.
"I will show the Atlantic
once and for all
that I am the most beautiful place.

This means war!"

The mountain's thunderous words filled the air,
    and the wind blew them all the way to the sea.
    Upon hearing Katahdin's rage,
        the Atlantic answered, with a furl,

"You want war? I'll give you war.
    I will do anything to save my honor
    and place in the North!"

And so, at the same exact moment, the mountain
and the sea unleashed their fury toward each other.

Katahdin triggered its mightiest thunderstorms,
most frigid blizzards,
and strongest avalanches
and hurled them at the Atlantic.

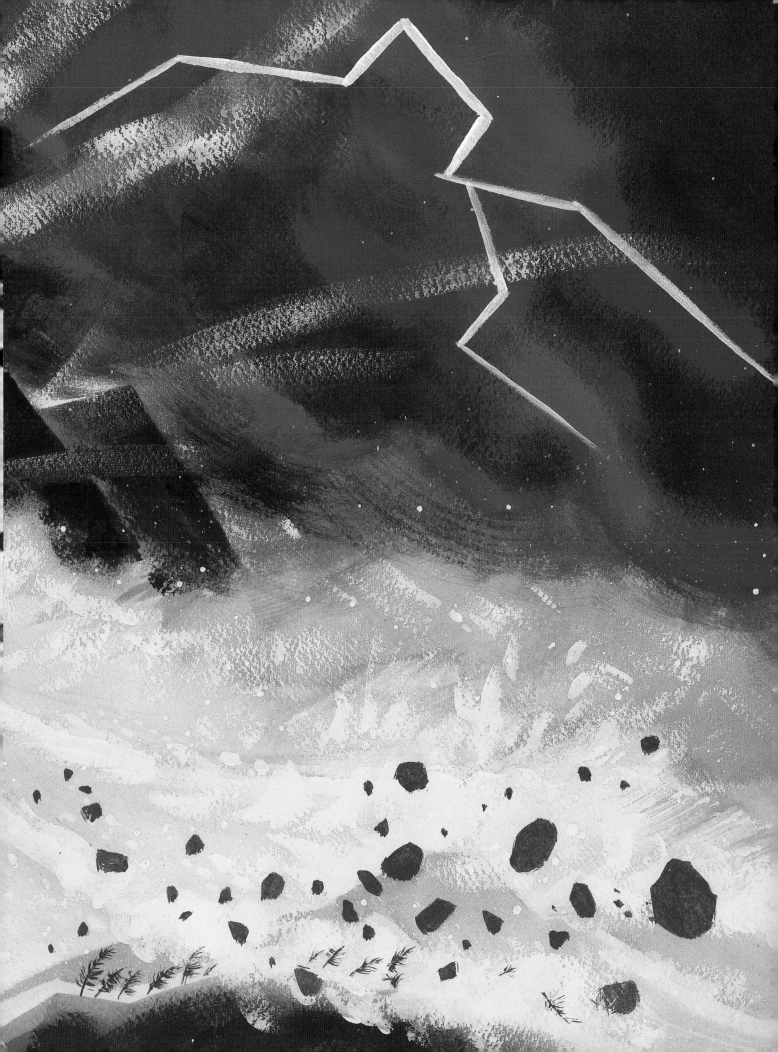

The Atlantic fired its flooding waters,
wildest waves, and harshest hurricanes
and blasted them toward Katahdin.

And when, at last, the fighting stopped
    and all was quiet, the mountain and the sea
    had not reached each other with their attacks.

But all the North Land between them
was barren, destroyed.

For the first time,
    Katahdin and the Atlantic
    could *see* each other
    across the North Land.

They stared in awe.

Both gasped,
    "You truly *are* beautiful,
        so different . . .
    but magnificent.
        Spectacular!

I am so sorry
    I doubted you."

From that day on,
Katahdin and the
Atlantic pledged
to work together for the
good of the North Land.

And slowly, over many, many seasons,
the snows melted from atop the mountain's peak
and drained from mountain springs
to brooks to rivers
and flowed, flowed, flowed
all the way to the Atlantic Ocean.

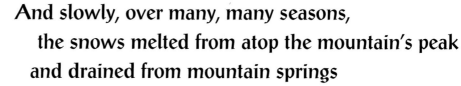

And so, at last, the beauty of the mountain
and the beauty of the sea were connected.

In fact, the forests and the fields of the in-between lands
grew greener, more lush than they had ever been before.
It was as if the new bond between the great mountain
and the great ocean was so strong that it spread
their wondrous beauty in all directions.

And so, long ago, before people lived in
the North Land, Katahdin and the Atlantic Ocean
had the first feud—over a misunderstanding.
But in time, they realized their mistake,
gave up their anger, and healed all they had destroyed—
creating the North Land the world knows today.

THE END